ON YOUR KNEES

STEPHANIE PERRY MOORE

#2

THE *SWOOP* LIST

ON YOUR KNEES

STEPHANIE PERRY MOORE

darbycreek

MINNEAPOLIS

Darby Creek
A division of Lerner Publishing Group, Inc.
241 First Avenue North
Minneapolis, MN 55401 USA

For reading levels and more information, look up this title at
www.lernerbooks.com.

Cover: © Luba V Nel/Dreamstime.com (woman); © Andrew Marginean/
Dreamstime.com (brick wall); © Andrew Scherbackov/Shutterstock.com
(notebook paper).

Interior: © Andrew Marginean/Dreamstime.com (brick hall background);
© Sam74100/Dreamstime.com, pp. 1, 41, 79; © Luba V Nel/Dreamstime.
com, pp. 10, 49, 87; © iStockphoto.com/kate_sept2004, pp. 18, 57, 93;
© Hemera Technologies/AbleStock.com/Thinkstock, pp. 26, 64, 101;
© Rauluminate/iStock/Thinkstock, pp. 34, 72, 109.

Main body text set in Janson Text LT Std 12/17.5.
Typeface provided by Adobe Systems.

Library of Congress Cataloging-in-Publication Data

Moore, Stephanie Perry.
    On your knees / by Stephanie Perry Moore.
        pages cm. — (The Swoop List ; #2)
    Summary: Determined to turn their presence on the "Swoop List" into
a positive thing, five Georgia high school girls face new challenges at home
and in school by believing in something greater than themselves, especially
their friendship.
        ISBN 978-1-4677-5805-5 (lib. bdg. : alk. paper)
        ISBN 978-1-4677-6050-8 (pbk.)
        ISBN 978-1-4677-6192-5 (EB pdf)
        [1. Conduct of life—Fiction. 2. Interpersonal relations—Fiction.
3. Dating (Social customs)—Fiction. 4. High schools—Fiction.
5. Schools—Fiction. 6. Sex—Fiction.] I. Title.
    PZ7.M788125On 2015
    [Fic]—dc23   2014025729

Manufactured in the United States of America
1 – SB – 12/31/14

For
my beaus,

Samuel Brown
Fred Bryant
Oscar Byrd
Malik Dawkins
Seth Fallen
Anthony Glover
Aaron Heyward
Dorian Lee
Angelo Matos
Brandon Roberts
Zachary Shelton
Cedric Trussell

You are true gentlemen destined
for greatness.
Stay on your knees
so that God can take you soaring!

CHAPTER ONE

Cohesively (Sanaa's Beginning)

"They might be calling us h-o-e-s, but you know *where* they're calling us that?" Willow Dean boldly stated, shocking the other four swoop girls at their slumber party. "Not to our faces, that's where. And why y'all looking at me like I said something wrong? That's what they're calling us. We might as well embrace it. Come on, Sanaa, right?"

Sanaa Mathis was completely different from Willow. Willow was brass. Sanaa was calm-spirited. But this last month had made her tougher than she'd ever had to be before, so she nodded, agreeing with Willow. People might be talking about them, but they weren't doing it to their faces anymore. The camaraderie that they had formed shut Jackson High School's bullies, haters, and wannabes up. Sanaa didn't want to admit that she was now deemed "easy" by her peers. But she was done with being depressed with a list she could not change.

A month prior, some jerks anonymously wrote a list called "The Swoop List" that held the names of the top five girls in the school who were considered easy. Someone took a photo of the list and put it online. Pretty much everyone at school had seen it now. Sanaa had only been with her boyfriend, Miles. Nobody knew Miles was her man because her best friend, Toni, liked him. Toni had asked Sanaa to talk to Miles on her behalf. Miles wasn't interested in Toni, though. He was interested in Sanaa, and Sanaa fell for Miles too. Since Sanaa couldn't break her girlfriend's heart, as the attraction grew between Sanaa and Miles, she convinced him to keep it a secret.

However, when the list was revealed, Toni started playing mind games, telling Sanaa that somebody had put her on the list, so maybe it was the guy she was sleeping with. Sanaa didn't know Toni knew she had a guy. The two of them hadn't been as tight for the past month since the list came out.

Sanaa was even more confused when, soon after the swoop list had been released, she caught Miles in Toni's arms. Or maybe it was the other way around. It just caught Sanaa so completely off guard that she hadn't spoken to him in weeks. Toni hadn't reached out to her either, and usually Sanaa was the one always kissing Toni's behind. Not anymore. Not since Sanaa had been getting counsel from Ms. Davis, the best guidance counselor in the whole wide world, who'd connected all the girls on the list.

Even though they were from varied backgrounds—Willow Dean, a preacher's kid who was the most promiscuous; Olive Bell, a foster girl who had been hanging with gang members to make ends meet; Octavia Streeter, the redhead whom Sanaa was still trying to figure out; and Pia Alvarez, the shy Hispanic girl— they still bonded great. Now they were having a slumber party at Willow's house. It'd been a rough few weeks for all of them. They leaned on each other for support.

Sanaa's heart had stopped moments earlier when Pia actually tried to take her own life with a bunch of pills in the bathroom. It wasn't just the swoop list weighing Pia down. She had been raped, gotten pregnant, and had an abortion. Sanaa realized that, compared to Pia, her life wasn't so upside down. If she could tell Pia to hang on, she had to hang on and be strong too.

"Yeah, y'all, Willow's right. We've got to embrace this whole swoop list thing. We wore the sweatshirts today. Everybody knows now we aren't taking them or the list seriously. They can label us, but we must embrace the label, swoop in, and clean up our lives like we said we were going to do. We will come out better from this whole experience. Willow's right. They're calling us names, but not to our faces anymore."

"I'm just saying, if another one does," Willow said, standing up, "it's on."

Sanaa didn't want to be the leader of the group. Willow wanted that title, but because she was so vocal, the other three girls looked to Sanaa, and she knew they thought of her as a leader. Willow's phone vibrated, and she immediately got up and dashed away.

"Sometimes she's so strong," Olive said, looking uncomfortable. "I just wonder if all that's real."

"Yeah," Octavia added. "Willow makes us all think she has it so together, but I believe she's breaking too."

Pia said, "I agree. You definitely should go check on her, Sanaa, because when I was in that bathroom, if you guys hadn't come and checked on me . . . who knows?"

"Well, I don't think she's going to try to harm herself," Sanaa voiced. Then she locked her gaze with Pia's and added, "I guess you never know."

Sanaa went into the hallway, trying to find Willow. It was Willow's house, and Sanaa wasn't used to walking around in unfamiliar places, so she called out, "Willow! Willow!"

"She went that way," a younger guy came out into the hallway and said. "I'm her brother, Will."

Sanaa felt weird seeing the young guy stare. "Well, it was nice to meet you."

Will blocked her path. "Willow don't have too many friends. I'm surprised she's having a sleepover. Our parents were too. Y'all know you gotta go to church tomorrow."

"Church? Huh?" Sanaa asked, all confused.

"Yup. Willow ain't told you that part? That was the condition of my mom letting y'all stay."

"I don't think any of us brought anything to wear."

"We got teen church. You can wear jeans. No excuses. But if you give me a smooch, I'll tell my mom to let y'all sleep in. She loves me. She hates Willow," the brat stepped closer and said with bad breath and all.

Sanaa put her hand over her mouth, and Willow shouted out, "Leave my friend alone!" Willow appeared out of nowhere, yanked Sanaa into the bathroom, and slammed the door.

"Sorry about my brother."

"No, no, thanks for rescuing me."

"He's a wannabe. I told him he needs to sit down somewhere and grow some muscles."

"He told me about church," Sanaa revealed in an unpleasant voice.

"Oh yeah, yeah, yeah, I was going to tell y'all about that."

"We have to go?"

"Yeah," Willow said. "Sorry, but it's quick. Hey, check out this!"

Willow showed Sanaa the text. It read,

Dearest swoop girl.

Now that you've been called out and you guys have come together, don't think that's all you need to do. That's a great first step and all, but I know from firsthand experience this is just the beginning. Even though I'm not with y'all, I see y'all. You don't want to go out like me. Get down on your knees and fix your heart. I'm just saying. You're an angel.

Love, Leah.

Sanaa had first found out she was on the swoop list from a letter from Leah taped to her locker. The creepy thing was that the letter had been written on Leah's obituary, clipped out of a newspaper. Sanaa and the other swoop girls didn't really know who Leah was.

"Why's a dead girl writing us? Who's sending us this crap?" Willow asked, but Sanaa had no clue.

Then Sanaa's phone went off. Though Sanaa was leery, she told Willow not to sweat it and assured her they'd talk about it later. Then she handed Willow back her phone, so she could take Toni's call.

When Sanaa was alone, she said, "Hello."

"So you can't call nobody?" Toni huffed rudely.

"The phone works both ways," Sanaa uttered, not backing down.

"Well, I'm calling you now. Where are you, anyway?"

Sanaa didn't really think that was any of Toni's business, so she didn't answer.

"Oh, you hanging out with them heifers? Whatever. You'll see hanging out with them is only going to worsen your reputation, not make it better. You know that, right?" Toni badgered.

"Bye, Toni," Sanaa said, and hung up the

phone before she said something to truly hurt Toni's feelings.

Sanaa leaned her head against the hall wall. When she didn't come back for a few minutes, the other swoop girls came out and saw she was upset. She walked farther down the hall for solace, but they wouldn't leave her alone.

"Don't even ask. People aren't going to understand this group of ours, ya know. But I'm okay with that because you guys are real. Screw what they think," Sanaa declared, being brash like Willow. She hugged the swoop girls. "We're bonding and jelling cohesively."

CHAPTER TWO

Disappointedly (Willow's Beginning)

Willow felt bad that Sanaa was sad. The well-being of all the swoop list girls weighed heavy on her. They were having fun at the slumber party, but a lot of emotions had come out too. All this concern made Willow unable to sleep that night.

For the first time in a long time, Willow was thankful to go to church the next morning. She needed her mom to give her a word of encouragement. She dared not let her mom know that. Willow knew that she would be one of the biggest sinners in the place. But it wasn't just about her anymore. She'd been on the dance team and had a cool relationship with a female or two, but she never had any best friends. This was something new she was feeling with the swoop list girls. They hadn't even been connected that long, but she didn't want any of them in pain.

She wanted to hug Sanaa and tell her, "Forget your best friend. She is tripping. You don't need her anyway. I'll replace her." But she refrained from saying that because it would be too presumptuous. She wanted to tell Olive, "I'm glad you're leaving the gang member alone. You must be blind if you don't see your foster brother wants to be your man." But she didn't want to pry. She also thought about telling Octavia, "I know you're white and all, but you're the coolest white chick I've ever met. Quit being a doormat. Stand up to some of these black folks around here who are all bark and no bite." But she didn't really want Octavia to stand up to her, so she didn't offer that piece of advice. And then there was Pia. Sweet Hispanic Pia, who actually was the most truthful with them all. Deep pain makes you vulnerable. Willow simply wanted to tell her, "It's gonna be okay." However, Willow didn't really know if she could get over what Pia was going through if it had happened to her, so she said nothing.

Willow wanted to earn their trust. She knew the best thing she could do was get them to church, and not just because her mom made that a condition for having the sleepover. No. She knew her mother was prophetic. Willow believed hearing a great word would uplift them all.

An hour and a half later, they were all sitting in church. Willow's mother preached, "There is no problem that faith can't solve. Whether your boss is tripping, your parents are tripping, or your peers at school are tripping, there is One who sits on high and looks down low and wants to heal the deepest sinner. And let he who is without sin cast the first stone. If we each take care of our own house, clean up our own home, and get our own hearts straight, then life will be better. It's good when you can have friends on this earth to walk with you through the turmoil. But it's even better when you can look above and know when no one else is there, He is."

Willow wasn't trying to push her religion on any of the other four girls. They hadn't even talked about if they believed in anything. Everybody was just kind enough to go because that was Willow's mom's requirement. Thankfully, Willow could tell as their heads nodded and some tissues were pulled out to wipe tears that all four of them enjoyed it. But she knew, regardless of if they got something out of the message or not, she was sure changed by it.

"I hope my mama wasn't too boring," Willow said, not wanting to assume the message was okay.

"Are you kidding? That was right on time!" Sanaa smiled and said.

"I don't have to have a heavy heart. I can just give it to Him. I don't know when was the last time I was in church," Olive voiced with sincerity. "But being here today, I know I need to go more often. Your mom was good."

"What she said," Octavia uttered and laughed as she pointed at Olive.

"I'm Catholic, but this nondenominational thing was right on time this morning," Pia told her.

Just as Willow was about to smile bright, proud that her mom had blessed them all, Hillary, her nemesis from the dance team stepped up to her and said, "If it isn't the swoop sluts . . . oops, I'm in church. I probably shouldn't say that. But Lord knows the truth is the light."

"What are you even doing here? You don't attend here," Willow huffed.

Rolling her eyes, Hillary said, "Neither do they. I'm a guest this morning. Is that alright? Or you think you own the building like you own all the boys you slept with?"

"Come on, Willow," Olive said, sensing the drama brewing. "Don't even waste your time."

"Yeah, you better listen!" Hillary blurted out.

Olive tried to pull Willow away, but Willow jerked her hand back and stepped back to Hillary, yelling, "What? You want a piece of this? You jealous or something, wench?"

"Jealous of your stank behind? Uh, no!"

"So why you always startin' something? Is there something you want from me?"

"I want you to get off the dance team."

"That ain't gonna happen!" Willow declared.

"It needs to! You bringing us down. You know there are over sixty guys at our school who are saying they've been with you? That's nasty, and you probably think it's so cool."

"Come on, Willow, don't let her get under your skin." Olive yelled out, but Willow wasn't hearing it.

Hillary egged on, "No, let her go! You can't dispute the truth. You can put on your little church clothes instead of the revealing stuff you walk around school in, get some new little friends who are in the same slutty boat as you, sleeping with every Tom, Dick, and Harry. And if you think that's gon' make you not what you are, then keep dreaming, because you're nothing but a—"

Before Hillary could utter any words of profanity, Willow ran over and socked her in the nose. In Willow's eyes, Hillary had it coming. A smirk of pleasure filled Willow's face.

"Oh my gosh!" Hillary squealed. "Look, blood! What'd you do to me?"

"Nothing your tail didn't deserve!" Willow said, standing over her and wanting to hit her even more.

Suddenly, Willow's mom appeared and asked, "What is going on here?"

"Your daughter. She broke my nose!" Hillary yelled.

"I didn't break anything!" Willow screamed back.

Willow's mom went over and checked the girl's face. She called over some other people in the church and got them to take Hillary away to make sure she was okay. Displeasure was all in Willow's mom's face.

In front of the crowd, her mother scoffed, "I can't believe this. You come to church and you fight? With everything I have to put up with you, Willow, I don't deserve such disrespect."

"But Mom, you don't know what she was saying about me. You don't know, but she started it!"

"Did she put her hands on you, Willow?"

"No, but she was instigating the tension."

"And? We've talked about this so many times." She exhaled. "I'm not trying to get upset with you right here after I just preached, Willow, but it's just one thing after another with you. Assaulting somebody? That's crazy."

Willow wanted to cry. She hated that some group of guys had put their names on the swoop list. She hated that someone had made her so angry that she punched that person on hallowed ground. She hated that she'd let her mom down. She hated that the woman she loved was now looking at her so disappointedly.

CHAPTER THREE
Catastrophically (Olive's Beginning)

As soon as Olive entered the foster home, the younger kids who lived there rushed up to her. After a long night away, she realized, though her home was nontraditional, she had a family. Olive embraced the kids.

"Where've you been? Charles has been worried sick," said Dazia, a little girl who was in the third grade.

Petey, a little boy in the fifth grade, said, "He sure has. Bugging me every five minutes 'bout where you are."

"We're about to go to the movies with

Ms. B. Come with us," Dazia said, tugging on Olive's shirt.

"Where are Charles and Shawn?" Olive asked.

"Back that way," Petey pointed.

"You two have fun with Ms. B. I'll make sure the big boys stay in line, cool?"

The two younger ones gave Olive sad faces, but smiled when she tickled them as she walked past to check on the older boys. Olive ran into Ms. B. Her foster mother was such a lovely woman. If she wasn't almost a hundred, Olive would ask her to be adopted. She was actually seventy-nine, but to Olive, that was old. Olive wanted to talk to her so bad. But the last thing she wanted to do was burden Ms. B, because she hadn't been feeling too well, and Olive was happy she was going out with the kids to a movie.

Ms. B hugged Olive. "Hey there, sweetie. I know those kids blabbed about our outing. You don't want to go with us? You back just in time."

"No, ma'am. I've got some homework to do."

"Well, I'm glad you enjoyed yourself this weekend, basketball games, girls' sleepovers, and you went to church this morning. I'm proud of you losing the attitude, talking about ma'am. You're turning into a fine young lady. We'll be on back. Keep an eye out for me on them boys. They hot mad 'bout something."

"Will do."

Ms. B's son used to come on Sunday afternoons to pick her and the kids up and take them on outings. They'd go bowling, skating, and finally, after a month's hiatus, they were going to the movies. The kids would always ask Olive to go, and she'd always say no. Now Olive was starting to appreciate and understand that she needed to accept being with the people who cared about her. She made a mental note that next time she'd go with them.

Hearing noises from the boys' room, Olive quickly hurried to the back of the house to see what was going on with Charles and Shawn. Why did Ms. B say they were all upset?

"There you are. Thought you weren't coming back," Charles rudely said, standing near the dresser.

Charles wasn't looking at Olive, but she knew

there was a little bit more to the rant he was giving. Shawn was snickering. Olive didn't want to face the facts that she was having some serious feelings for her foster brother, but that was the truth. And it did seem like a two-way street since Charles was upset that she had been gone. There could only be one reason why he cared. He used to say she got on his nerves, but now he wanted her around. He liked her too.

"I hope you had fun, at least," Charles uttered sarcastically when she didn't respond to his first statement.

Olive saw Charles was salty. She went over and stood by him. She gave him a bump, hip-to-hip.

"He want you to bump him alright," Shawn joked.

"Whatever, hush, man," Charles snarled.

"What's going on with y'all? Ms. B said you two were mad about something."

Charles hit the dresser. "It's that punk Tiger. He won't let it go; he keeps starting stuff. I'm going to have finish it, though. Word's out he gon' take me."

Panicked, Olive said, "What? We need to leave and go to the police! Where did he say that? You've got it written down?"

"I told you you shouldn't tell her, man," Shawn said.

"You right," Charles agreed, then he went over to Olive. "Don't worry. We got this."

With eyes watering, she said, "Y'all got what? You don't own no guns."

Charles went over to a drawer and pulled out a silver handgun.

"You got a loaded gun in this house with those kids?" Olive said, outraged.

"Naw, girl," Shawn said, and he reached in another drawer, got some bullets, and threw them to Charles.

"You've got to put that up, Charles. We've got to get rid of that thing."

Before she could say any more, Charles came over to her and kissed her passionately. "If he threatens me, I can deal with it, Olive, but if he threatens you, he's dead."

Stunned and floored, she grabbed him and said, "Let me handle Tiger."

"You kidding? I can't believe you dated him as long as you did. You looked the other way about his crimes. I know for a fact he done took a sucker out with you around. You can't handle him. Can you?" Charles asked.

Olive looked the other way. She remembered the night exactly. A guy owed Tiger some money. That guy didn't want to get in trouble, so he brought another guy who owed him to Tiger. Olive sat in the car, but he heard screams, wails, and then dead silence. Tiger and two of his thugs, plus the guy, went in, but only three of them came out. Tiger was wiping off a bloody knife when he got back in the car. Olive never said anything. People heard about it. Tiger loved to brag, and the fact that Charles knew made her own blood turn cold in her veins.

"Why did you kiss me?" she asked, needing not to think about the impending danger.

"Yeah, man, why'd you kiss her?" Shawn teased, still surprised his buddy took action.

"Get out!" Charles teased Shawn back.

Shawn gave a nod of approval. "I'ma play Xbox in the living room anyway. Let me know when you're ready to ride out and take this jerk."

"He's not going anywhere!" Olive said.

"I'll be up in a sec," Charles told Shawn.

When Shawn left, Charles packed the gun and bullets. Olive said, "And how y'all going, anyway?"

"Ms. B left us the keys to her car."

"She didn't tell you to drive it."

"She didn't say we couldn't."

Charles put down his bag and put his arms around Olive's waist. She put her hands to her lips and felt them, not believing what she felt earlier was real. Reading her mind, he kissed her lips again to reassure her. He was so sensual, and he felt so good. It was completely different from anything she'd ever felt with Tiger.

Olive questioned, "Why are you doing this? I just got out of a crazy relationship."

"And . . . I can't get you out of my dreams, Olive. Tell me you feel something."

Just when he went to kiss her again, they heard shots ringing out through the house. Charles got Olive down as debris started flying everywhere. Olive's heart was racing, and it felt like it went on for hours, but it was only probably five minutes of utter chaos.

When the madness stopped, Olive asked Charles, "Are you okay?"

Charles stood, helped her up, and dusted them both off. "I'm gonna get that son of a . . ."

"No, calm down. I'm fine. Wait, where's Shawn?" Olive said, wondering why he hadn't rushed in.

"Shawn!" Charles shouted.

Both of them rushed to the front of the house when Shawn didn't respond. Olive's fears were realized when they saw Shawn lying on the floor, not moving. Olive collapsed catastrophically.

CHAPTER FOUR
Fearfully (Octavia's Beginning)

When Octavia entered the school building the first Monday of February, she was all smiles. She'd been a loner for so long, but now the red-head was blossoming like a rose in the spring. She wouldn't have to walk through the halls alone, and she'd never been more excited to get to school than she was that particular morning.

Octavia hated that she didn't have a cell phone and couldn't afford one. From time to time she had a prepaid one. That's when months were good for her father. Last month hadn't been a good month for her dad, so she didn't have a phone to check in with her friends. Therefore, she hoped the girls hadn't moved their meet-up location, because she had been standing there for about ten minutes, but there was no sign of Sanaa, Willow, Olive, or Pia.

As other students were staring at her, looking at their cell phones and covering their mouths, Octavia thought maybe another swoop list had come out. At the very least, she felt something big was going on. When she truly studied the crowd, she realized folks seemed serious. More of them looked at their phones, but no laughing ensued.

Wanting to know what was up, Octavia went over to a stranger and said, "What are y'all looking at?"

"There was a shooting at a group home last night. I think somebody died."

There was only one group home in Jackson. Octavia's heart stopped. What if something had happened to Olive? Was that where the swoop list girls were?

"Could I borrow your cell phone?" Octavia said to the guy she'd never met. "What's your name?"

He squinted and replied, "It's Ben, and no, I don't know you."

"Please, Ben? I'm sure you got an unlimited calling plan. I'm not going anywhere with it. It's an emergency. I know somebody who lives at that house. Do you know who got shot?"

"The news just said a teenager," Ben said.

"Please, let me borrow your phone for a second," Octavia said in a panicked voice as she snatched the phone away.

"Hey!" Ben yelled as Octavia held up one finger, pleading for a second.

Octavia opened up her notebook. Right on the inside cover were all the girls' numbers. She started dialing Sanaa's number immediately.

"Who is this?" Sanaa asked, not recognizing the digits.

"It's me, Octavia. I borrowed somebody's phone."

"Oh my gosh, girl. Where you at?"

"I thought we were meeting in front of the school," Octavia said.

"Girl, that was last week. We changed it. Come over by the cafeteria. Hurry, I need to tell you something. It's not good, Octavia."

Clutching her chest, Octavia asked, "Is it true? Is Olive dead?"

"Just come!" Sanaa shouted before hanging up.

Sensing the worst, Octavia took off. She still had Ben's phone in hand. He noticed and sprinted after her.

Ben threw his keys at her back, and she stopped.

"You got my phone!" he yelled.

"Ouch!" Octavia said, noticing the phone still in her hand. "Oh, I'm sorry."

"See, that's why I don't let folks use it," Ben said, holding his hand out.

"I'm sorry!" She handed it to him and quickly went to the cafeteria. Before she could get there, she ran into Ms. Davis. Octavia asked, "Do you know what's going on?"

In a calm voice, Ms. Davis said, "One of our students was shot last night."

"I know, at the group home. But word's out someone is dead." Octavia's eyes held panic.

Ms. Davis touched her shoulder. "No, nobody's dead."

"So Olive is okay?"

"No, sweetie," Ms. Davis said emphatically.

Octavia looked confused. "So she's hurt bad?"

"Calm down. It's not Olive. But I'm so glad you girls are bonding."

And then, as relieved as Octavia was, a knot grew in her throat. "Wait, was it Charles or Shawn?"

Ms. Davis's eyes started watering. When it took her too long to answer, Octavia started sprinting again. She ran to the cafeteria to see her girls.

"We were about to leave you," Willow said when she reached them.

"I got held up with Ms. Davis. Where's Olive?"

"She didn't come to school today. She's at the hospital."

"Is it Charles? I know she's devastated," Octavia uttered. All the girls hung their heads down low. "Somebody talk to me! Who was shot?"

Sanaa put her arm around Octavia. There was nothing official confirming that Octavia and Shawn had something going on, but everyone at school knew they were the cutest, newest white couple around Jackson High School. Sanaa, Willow, and Pia didn't know how to tell her that Shawn was injured badly and barely hanging on to life.

Octavia stomped and blurted out, "Please don't sugarcoat anything for me. Just tell me. I can tell the way y'all are looking at me—it's Shawn. Ms. Davis said the person is not dead, but she couldn't say if they'd be alright. Is he gonna make it?" They didn't answer. "I gotta get to the hospital."

"That's where we're going right now," Sanaa said as she turned to exit the building. Willow, Pia, and Octavia followed.

The four of them didn't care about cutting school. They only cared about being there for their friends. When they pulled into the hospital parking lot, Olive was waiting. Sanaa couldn't park soon enough. They all got out and hugged Olive. Tears fell from them all. They could only imagine the horrendous ordeal that Olive had been through. To be in your home and have gunfire ring out seemed crazy to them all.

"I don't know how I made it," Olive said in a devastated tone.

"You okay, though?" Octavia asked and she hugged Olive. "I'm so glad you're okay, but what about Shawn? Is he going to live?"

"I'm so scared for him," Olive said as she stepped back. "His blood kept gushing out of his side. He was just lying there. He wouldn't move. It was taking the ambulance forever. I swear it seemed like his entire insides were lying on the floor."

"What!" Willow screamed out as she touched Octavia's back.

Olive said, "Yeah, but I think that was just my mind."

"Don't scare us like that," Sanaa said.

"So is he gonna be okay?" Octavia screamed.

Pia chimed in, "Yeah, please tell us something, especially for Octavia."

Olive shared, "The bullet actually went in the front of his stomach and through his back. Thankfully, it was more on his side."

The other four girls did not understand how this was good news. Octavia practically keeled over, unable to deal with any of this. Olive noticed her sincere concern for Shawn.

Olive wanted to ease the worry, so she explained, "Listen, the bullet could have lodged inside his body and stayed put. I'ma be honest: we don't know, but he's a fighter. He hasn't come to, but he's stable. We gotta believe he's gonna pull through. They're telling us it's touch and go."

Octavia wanted to fall to the ground. She did stumble a bit and was caught by Sanaa. She was so out of it, she couldn't even tell who caught her. After all the girls got her back to being coherent, Octavia realized she deeply cared for this guy, Shawn. Replaying the words *touch and go* in her mind over and over had her deeply concerned, truly and fearfully.

CHAPTER FIVE

Heavyheartedly (Pia's Beginning)

Pia was so sick and tired of being sick and tired. She was still sore from the abortion procedure. She was very tired of continuing to beat herself up for something she felt was best. And now, added on to her personal pain, as much as the swoop girls were trying to make her smile, this recent shooting was too much to bear. When the five girls showed up back at school after skipping part of the day, the attendance officer sent them straight to the office. Thankfully, the principal knew they were meeting with Ms. Davis and told them to head to her.

"Girls, you can't leave school. I saw Octavia

earlier this morning, and I knew she was upset. And Olive I know you live with the young man who was shot, but girls—"

Olive cut in and said, "But Ms. Davis, there is no 'but.' He is hanging on, and we only left after the doctor came out and told us it looks like he is going to be okay. I wasn't going to leave, but Ms. B, my foster mother, has been texting me with updates. They can kick me out of school if they think it wasn't right for me to skip. I needed to check on him."

"Same with us. We're friends with him also," Octavia added.

All of the girls started fussing with Ms. Davis, needing her to understand why they broke the rules. She wasn't going to cosign on their decision, but she agreed to make sure this time they were excused. As they all hugged her, Pia sat melancholy. Ms. Davis told the other girls to go on to their last period. She wanted to talk to Pia alone.

"I'm really worried about her," Pia heard Sanaa say to Ms. Davis. "She might need psychological help."

Once they were alone, Ms. Davis turned her full attention to Pia. "Talk to me, Pia, tell me what's wrong."

Pia just sat there as if she didn't have a tongue. There was so much inside of her that she wanted to say. She also wanted to scream. She needed the hurt to go away.

"I promise you'll feel better if you let it out," Ms. Davis said in a patient and caring voice.

"I'm a murderer, okay! There! How am I supposed to deal with that? You know I was raped, and I ended up pregnant, my mom didn't want me to keep the baby, and honestly I didn't want to keep it either, so I didn't. Now I'm having nightmares. I feel like I'm being haunted. And why do I deserve to live when I didn't let my baby have the same privilege?"

"I'm not here to judge you. You and your mother decided what you all felt was the best course of action. Because you're having a hard time dealing with that, I want to see you through. You can't carry this burden around. It's done. So you've got to make peace with it. Let it go."

"How do you make peace with the fact that the baby that was growing inside of me is gone?"

"You concentrate on moving forward. And all we can do in life sometimes is to let ourselves off the hook and go and be better than the mistakes we feel we've made. You can't change the past, but you can shape your future."

Those positive words hit Pia in her heart and gave her the strength she needed. She hugged Ms. Davis. The talk didn't change the facts, but it did change her thought process. She now had to decide to be stronger and move forward with her life. She only hoped she could.

"I can give you a pass to class, or you can sit here for a minute—the last bell is about to ring. You going home?"

"No, ma'am. Since the basketball team is doing so well and we're going to the play-offs, I've got cheer practice. I don't feel like it, but hearing what you've shared, I need to push myself through."

Ms. Davis smiled. "That's what I'm talking about. Have faith. And I'm here any time."

Pia didn't know how to respond to that, so she didn't. She just grabbed her things and headed to the gym. As she walked, she saw tons of signs about the upcoming Valentine's Day dance. She wondered, how could the world be so happy when she felt so miserable? Trying to remember Ms. Davis's words, she took a deep breath and walked on.

She wasn't usually in the gym so early. Since Ms. Davis didn't make her go to her last class, she got there before the end-of-the-day bell rang. A lot of the basketball players were hanging out. They had weight training as their last class. Immediately, Pia slowed upon hearing male voices before she rounded the corner.

She heard one guy joke, "It's time to catch another girl off guard. We've been playing good ever since that night we took it. Can we do Pia again?"

"That sweet shakida turns me on when I look at her. She's not like the sisters wearing weave. Pia's long, flowing hair does something to a brother."

Another bragged, "Yeah, I want to put my

hands all through it too, but this time I want to let her see who I am. You know she probably liked it. It's not like she put up a big fuss."

All Pia had to do was round the corner, and she would be able to clearly view the three guys who raped her. But she couldn't move. It was like somebody was actually holding her back or like she was tied down. She wanted to break free. She wanted to hurt the world. Instead, she ran into the boys' locker room. It was dark, and she hit the metal trash can. She looked inside and saw a bunch of trash. She scrambled through her purse and grabbed the book of matches. Pia took a match out, struck it, and threw it into the trash can. The flames erupted.

"What is going on? Is that a fire?" A wet Stephen Garcia rushed out of the shower and asked, "Are you crazy?"

"No! You guys are crazy. Were you a part of it? Were you with them?"

"With who?"

"Don't try and act all innocent like you don't know."

Stephen turned away. Any other time Pia

might have been interested in his naked butt, but all she wanted was to take her boot and kick him right in his crack. He turned around quickly as the flames started bustling over the top of the can. He grabbed a wet towel to cover the can, dousing the flames.

"Your teammates raped me, Stephen, and I want them dead."

"Well, they ain't in here, and the only two people that's gonna die if a fire grows right this second is me and you. And we need to live. I know a little something about what you're talking about, and I guess I've been silent too long. This isn't an accident that I'm in here right now. You want to turn them in, I'll back you up."

Forgetting that Stephen was nude, she fell into his arms, thankful for his support. Mentally freaking out from all she'd heard and done, she sobbed heavyheartedly.

CHAPTER SIX

Immeasurably (Sanaa's Middle)

Sanaa stayed after school to make up a quiz she'd missed in physics class earlier that day when she and her girls ditched school to go to the hospital. She was actually pretty thankful Ms. Davis worked it out to make her time away excused because she was trying to get into college, to go somewhere and to become somebody. She needed to finish strong to accomplish that goal.

While she still wasn't sure what she wanted to be, her folks wanted her to pursue a prominent career. They didn't go to college, and neither did their parents, or their parents' parents. She'd be a first-generation college graduate if she kept on the path they had for her.

Sanaa kept thinking things could be worse. Though she was in a two-parent household that barely made ends meet, compared to Olive who had no parents, Sanaa didn't have anything to complain about. She just wanted to do her part so that she could go to school. She knew she'd have to get a scholarship because her parents certainly didn't have any credit to take out loans. She'd heard about the Hope Scholarship from Ms. Davis. To qualify for the Hope Scholarship, she had to have a 3.0 in her core classes. She had a 3.4, so she had a chance at the scholarship. She'd also always dreamed of going to the University of Georgia, but their qualifications were higher. If she didn't put the pedal to the metal and help herself out, that longtime dream was going to fade away.

Feeling confident that she'd aced the quiz, Sanaa headed on out to the parking lot and ran into Pia. She noticed her friend was still frazzled. Sanaa wanted to ask if the talk with Ms. Davis helped, but she decided not to pry.

"Can you take me home?" Pia asked.

"Yeah, sure. I'm up to talking too, if you want," Sanaa said, pressing anyway.

"Please, Sanaa, I don't want to say nothing." Sanaa noticed a guy near the school staring hard at Pia. "Okay, I see that guy over there staring at you. The basketball player, what's his name? The Hispanic one? Stephen?"

"Yeah Stephen . . . who cares?"

"Okay, I know we're just starting to become friends, but in my definition of the word, friendship is a two-way street. You scared the heck out of us at the slumber party when you said you didn't want to be here. The last couple of weeks you seemed like everything was okay. Then, all of a sudden, earlier today you were reclusive again."

"Reclusive? What does that even mean?"

As they got in the car, Sanaa said, "I'm trying to use some SAT words. It means to withdraw. Can't you tell by the context language I used what it means? We've gotta get ready for college."

"Oh, Sanaa. College, really?" Pia said in an exhausted tone.

"Yeah, don't you wanna go? You can't even measure what college does for your future."

"Nothing wrong with doing a trade," Pia said, squinting her eyes.

"I know. Hispanic folks ain't the only ones that do that line of work. My parents do too. My dad is a brick mason, and my mom does hair, so I wasn't trying to offend you. I'm just saying. I want better than what my parents had, don't you?"

"My mom can't even keep a job. She thinks senoritas are the hottest thing since Marilyn Monroe. The white men, black men, and Hispanic men all want her. She just lays down, and our bills get paid. So, yeah. I want more than my mom, but that doesn't mean college is gonna do it."

"What's your GPA?" Sanaa asked her as they drove.

"A 3.1."

"You qualify for the Hope Scholarship. There are tons of great schools in our state that you can go to."

"I wouldn't do great in anybody's college."

"I'm not trying to pressure you about your

future. I'm just sayin' from where I stand, your future looks bright. I can only imagine that you keep focusing on what happened to you, but I encourage you to turn your attention to what can happen for you."

Out of the blue, Pia said, "I'm just debating if I wanna turn the guys in. I know somebody who knows who they are, and I got a good hunch who they are too."

"I thought you told us you were blindfolded?"

"I was. But no denying the voices. I heard them bragging about it, saying they wanted to do it all again."

"Are you serious?"

"I wish I was joking. I wish all of this was a bad nightmare. But it's my reality, and I just don't want them to get off scot-free. However, if I bring it to the forefront, then I've got to live it all again. I don't even have any evidence. I watch *Law and Order: SVU.*"

"Having a witness sounds like you got evidence to me," Sanaa shared.

They pulled into Pia's place, and Pia hugged Sanaa hard. "Thank you for believing in me.

Somewhere along the line I gotta start believing in myself."

Twenty minutes later Sanaa pulled up at her own house, and she was shocked to see Miles's car there. She parked, jumped out, and abruptly said, "What are you doing here? What do you want?"

"I wanna talk to you," her boyfriend pleaded.

"Well, I haven't reached out. Clearly you can see that I don't want to talk to you." Sanaa shuddered, thinking of the last time she saw Miles—embracing her former best friend, Toni. Sanaa had stopped talking to him after that.

"I haven't been able to function, Sanaa."

"Why don't you call Toni to help you with that little problem?" Sanaa started walking away.

He ran and got in front of her. "Toni? That's what I've been trying to tell you. What you saw wasn't what it was."

"I got twenty-twenty vision."

"You gotta give me a chance to explain."

"I don't have to do anything," Sanaa said with attitude as she placed her hands on her hips.

"If you loved me you would."

"Maybe that's just it. Maybe I don't love you anymore. How could I still love a guy who sold me out the way you did? And then as soon as the world views me as damaged goods, you go and get with my best friend, the one who's wanted you all along."

"So you never wanted me?" Miles said as he stepped close to Sanaa and stroked her cheek. "I don't know what you think you know. Whatever. I know you saw Toni's arms around me, and yes, I ain't gon' try to hide it anymore. She came on to me really hard, but I told her no. She was tugging on me and acting a little drunk and weird. I don't know."

"Drunk? Really? We were at school, Miles. Toni doesn't drink."

"There's a lot about Toni you don't know."

"And how come you know it?"

"That's not even the point, Sanaa. I guess I'm saying she's real jealous of you. But I love you, baby. I wouldn't sell you out."

"So what are you saying? She put my name on the swoop list?"

"No, no, no. I'm not saying that. I don't know how anybody found out that we were together, but I just want you. Don't you want me too?" He stepped in real close, leaned down, and gave her a kiss she couldn't back away from. In her mind she wanted to tell him, *Get the heck away*, but in her heart she held him close. They still had a lot to work on, but she accepted his apology because she cared for him immeasurably.

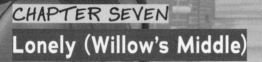

CHAPTER SEVEN

Lonely (Willow's Middle)

"So there's no need for you to walk in here, thinking you still on the dance team," Hillary said to Willow the next day after school.

"Girl, you better get out of my face! You would think you learned. I've already showed you that you don't run me."

"I don't run you, but I'm not in this alone. Booyah!" Hillary voiced as she held up a clipboard with a bunch of different signatures on it.

"What is this?" Willow said, snatching the clipboard out of Hillary's hand.

"It's a petition, dummy. Read the top carefully. It says, 'If you think only people with high moral standards should represent Jackson High in extracurricular activities, sign here to have Willow Dean removed from the dance team.'"

"Ha ha. Valentine's is coming up, not April Fools', my dear. You can't have me removed. Petition? That's whack." Willow laughed.

Hillary turned around to the squad standing behind her. "We've all signed it, everybody here."

"Everybody hasn't signed it," yelled out Willow's one friend, Carly, who had her back.

Willow rolled her eyes. "So what if you chumps signed a petition? I'm not going nowhere."

"Uh, we beg to differ. And why would you want to stay on a squad when you're the laughingstock of the school?" Hillary challenged.

Before things could heat up, the dance supervisor, Ms. Seely, called Willow to her office. With each step Willow had a bad feeling about what was taking place. Willow was shocked to see her mother seated in the office.

"So you're kicking me off for real?" Willow blurted before hearing them out.

Ms. Seely explained, "We do have a code of conduct that you signed and that your mom signed. I don't want to dig into your character, Willow. You're an awesome dancer, it's your senior year, we're headed to the play-offs, and I don't want to have to remove you. But there's some talk about your promoting bad behavior and maybe even punching one of the dance team members. If you can honestly tell me that all these allegations have no merit, then I say stay. But regardless of what you have or haven't done, it's a big distraction going on with you on this team. This is a team, not a solo, individual extracurricular activity."

Tearing up, Willow asked, "So what are you saying? I should take the high road and leave either way?"

"You're a tough cookie," Willow's mom said, and she touched her daughter's hand to give her strength. "And I'm proud that I raised you not to care what others think, but you admitted to me that there are some things that you want to clean up. We all need to get better, so I'm not condemning you. You know that, sweetie. But you don't have to stay in this hostile environment, either. You've got other talents and skills. You want to do some modeling or take some acting classes? Maybe we should try that?"

Snatching back her hand and wiping a tear that fell, Willow uttered, "So you want me to quit, Ma? You also taught me to never quit."

"Look at all these signatures, Willow. If this many people have a problem with something you're doing, though they're being petty, there's no need to take yourself through extra drama. But it's your decision. Ms. Seely is saying she'll support you either way," her mother said.

Willow looked at her mom. Though she was a pastor, she wasn't a lady who tolerated foolishness. The fact that Hillary had the audacity to even make up a list and get a bunch of people to sign it was insane. However, Willow knew she needed to give it credence. Hillary had gathered over two hundred signatures. Willow didn't want to be dancing and have people booing her. Though she probably could take it, she knew that kind of obsessive bullying could weigh on even the most confident of people.

Ms. Seely had asked her whether she'd broken the character clause of the contract she signed, and she probably wouldn't drill her for an answer, but Willow wasn't a liar. She wasn't a perfect angel. She had punched Hillary. And although Willow's appearance on the swoop list, after willingly sleeping with half the basketball team and the football team and a few sporadic guys in the school, didn't violate the contract, it had caused some problems on the team. Though it was subjective, Willow didn't want to be the one on trial anymore, so she looked at the two women who wanted her to take the easy way out. She obliged them.

"Can we go, Mom?"

Ms. Seely tried to give Willow a hug. Willow didn't want it. Her mom tried to comfort her. She didn't respond to that either. Carly waved bye. Willow just rolled her eyes. She had to give up something she loved because she didn't want to deal with the drama. But it still hurt.

Still, something in her was changing. The old Willow would have sought revenge and planned a way to get Hillary back. This new Willow understood that she really couldn't be mad at anybody but herself. While she didn't care what people thought of her, she realized she did want them to respect her. But how could they respect her when her actions hadn't been ones that respected herself? She'd punched a teammate. And, sure, she had loved it when guys placed their hands all on her and wanted to be with her.

But that was then, and this was now. Willow realized that those few moments of pleasure were not only potentially dangerous and unhealthy, but they also hadn't made her feel good about herself as a person. In the end, those moments made her feel unimportant and used. Those guys didn't care about her in an important, real way.

At home that night, Willow was in her bedroom when she heard a knock on her bedroom door.

"So, you up for some company?" Dawson said, peeking into her room.

Willow's mom didn't have any problem

with Dawson coming into her room since they'd grown up together. Her mom didn't realize that Dawson had real feelings for her, or maybe she did understand that and wanted Willow to appreciate a kind of guy who really cared versus the jerks she'd been with for so long. Nonetheless, he was there, but Willow didn't respond.

"Okay, then let me talk. I know a little bit about what's going on in your world. I've seen the petition come around the school. I actually tore one up. Maybe I shouldn't have told you that because it means there were more signatures you didn't see, but I got your back, front, and sides. If I could just sit with you for a minute until you are ready to talk, I'm cool with that."

She didn't yell for him to get out, but she didn't have anything to say either. She had no desire to call the swoop girls. She was actually a little salty with them, thinking at least one of them had to have seen the petition, but nobody told her. What kind of friends were they really? And she felt a little worthless. The tears started to drop. Dawson reached over and hugged her. She appreciated the moment of comfort because, thanks to him, though she couldn't express it, she didn't feel so lonely.

CHAPTER EIGHT

Martyrly (Olive's Middle)

"So you know Willow's pissed at us," Sanaa said to Olive over the phone the next evening.

"Why?" Olive asked, completely baffled. "We didn't do anything to her."

"Well, she called me, going off saying she couldn't believe we didn't tell her about the petition."

"Are you serious? We didn't tell her because we didn't wanna hurt her feelings. She finds out and she's mad at us anyway? I got way bigger problems to deal with than to be worried about somebody being too sensitive," Olive said.

"What's going on with you?"

"It's just Charles. He's planning to retaliate on Tiger."

Sanaa reminded her, "You can't let him. Tiger got his gang. They don't play fair. They got guns."

"And that's just it. Girl, Charles got one too."

Shocked, Sanaa said, "Oh my gosh, girl! You better make sure you don't get shot." There was a long pause. "You just gotta stay out of it, Olive."

"Sanaa, that's easy for you to say. None of this would even be happening if it wasn't for me. They're in here fixing my house, patching up bullet holes, because I was with the wrong guy. I can't just let Charles ruin his life trying to save mine."

"But then what if both you and Charles end up like Shawn, in the hospital or worse . . . you both end up dead? Then what?"

"Then I guess we'll both just be dead," Olive said nonchalantly. "But I can't live with anybody else getting hurt, and I'm not. I can't do it," Olive declared, and then she got hysterical. "Oh my gosh!"

"What?" Sanaa said, hearing Olive's panic.

"He's about to leave now!"

"Please stay out of it! Please! Just—"

"I'll call you back, okay?" Olive quickly hung up the phone. She ran out of the house, following Charles, who was clearly ready to settle a vendetta. "Charles, please, we need to talk about this."

"Olive, there's nothing to talk about! My boy is in the hospital."

"But, he's gonna be fine."

"But he almost wasn't fine. You and I both know that better than anybody. He was practically choking on his own blood, for goodness' sake."

"Oh, you're being dramatic!"

"I'm about to show your ex dramatic."

Olive got in front of Charles. "I'm not moving. I'm not leaving. I'm not letting you do this. You think Shawn would want you to go and face them guys on your own?"

"What you saying? I should wait until he's better and take care of it then? Nah. I'm not hearing that. I gotta go honor him."

"Where's the honor in fighting for him if you go and get yourself hurt?"

At that moment, Charles couldn't say a word. Olive was happy she had him silent. She needed to figure out what to say so that he would change his mind, follow her back inside, and cool down. The only thing she could think of to do to get him to chill was to share her real feelings. She didn't think she could have feelings for a guy anymore after Tiger completely used her up by letting all his boys hit it before dumping her, but she did. Since the day Tiger said "Hit the road" to Olive, Charles wanted to hit him. He actually did when they tussled in the cafeteria last month, which set these crazy, heated exchanges spiraling out of control. Olive knew Charles was her knight.

"What's all this ruckus about out here?" Ms. B came out of the house and yelled.

Charles gave Olive a look like *Don't you dare let her know what I'm about to do.*

"Oh, nothing," Charles said to her.

"Well, you need to go on and get to that store and get on back here. Be careful in my car now, baby, alright?" Ms. B told him.

"Yes, ma'am. Just some milk, that's all you need, right?" Charles asked in a sweet tone, not letting on his true intentions.

"You know what?" Ms. B said, thinking. "Go on and get me that bag of chips. And get Shawn some honey buns for when he gets back from the hospital. I gotta go to work tomorrow, but I at least want him to have some snacks. You got enough money, baby?"

"Yes, ma'am. I'll be right back."

Out of the blue, Olive said, "I'm going with him. Is that okay, Ms. B?"

"Yeah, that's good. It's late. You go with him, Olive honey."

It was written all over Charles's face that he did not want Olive going anywhere. However, she knew if she couldn't stop him from leaving, she had to go with him and try and stop him before he did something stupid. She ran inside, grabbed her purse, and headed to the door.

"So what you gonna do? Go to the grocery store and then go shoot? Or you gonna go shoot Tiger and then go to the grocery store?" Olive questioned after Ms. B closed the door.

"Okay, see you tryna be funny."

"Well, don't you see how ridiculous this all is?"

"I'm going to the grocery store, and that's where I'm going to leave you because I don't want nothing to go wrong."

"You think I'ma let you go by yourself? You can't do this, Charles. You can't!"

Suddenly Charles started yelling, "You can't tell me what I can't do! You don't know how it feels being threatened by Tiger and his chumps all the time. And then they gon' shoot up my house? The only thing I got to call home. It's bad enough I ain't really got one, and they gonna shoot up the foster home? They didn't know if those little kids was in there or if Ms. B was in there. They just gon' do what they gon' do and think there's no repercussions? Forget them! We're all okay, but they not gon' be okay."

"Charles, you can't. You can't!" Olive said as she searched his jacket for the gun, but when she found it, he snatched it away.

"It's loaded. Don't play. I'm about to tell

you I'm handling them, and if I have to shoot you, I will."

Olive looked at him with horror in her eyes, and he looked back at her, equally abrasive, and said, "I'm just saying. Stay out of my way. Ride if you gon' ride, but you can't stop me. I don't appreciate you trying to stop me from being martyrly."

CHAPTER NINE
Organically (Octavia's Middle)

Octavia came to school excited because this was the day Shawn was getting out of the hospital. She saw Willow and yelled, "Hey Willow, wait up!"

"For you? Please," Willow turned and rudely said to Octavia.

Octavia stood there, real confused. She didn't know why her new friend was angry at her. Before she could ask questions, Olive and Sanaa came up on both sides of her.

"She's tripping and not just mad at you. She's mad at all of us, thinking we didn't have her back," Olive explained.

Octavia sought clarity. "Have her back on what?"

"Did you see the petition that went around?" Sanaa asked.

"I didn't see it, but I remember us talking about it. We weren't going to tell her about it because we didn't want to hurt her feelings or anything."

"Exactly," Sanaa reminded.

"Well, I don't want her to be mad at me. I need to explain what we were thinking," Octavia uttered.

"She'll come around. Right now she just needs to cool down," Olive said. "Plus, I've got so much else on my mind. Shawn is coming home today, and I want to be there, but I'm here."

"I know we can't skip school again, but I can take you home right after school to get you there quicker than the bus," Octavia offered.

"That's great. Can you take Charles too?" Olive asked.

"Sure," Octavia said.

Sanaa squinted her eyes tight. "How are

you and Charles? How did all that play out yesterday?"

"I don't know how we are, considering he told me he was gonna kill me."

"What?" Sanaa squealed.

"Huh?" Octavia said.

Olive explained, "He wasn't playing, but as you see I'm still here. It's weird, though. He's mad at me because I basically told him he wasn't going to go and shoot up anybody."

"But threatening to shoot you, that's too much," Sanaa declared. "I almost came over to your place when you said he had a gun."

"You knew?" Octavia uttered.

"Yeah, I was on the phone with her when she was freaking out," Sanaa said. "Just glad you handled it. But if you're scared—"

"I'm fine," Olive said. "He apologized and settled the heck down. We just went to the grocery store and back home."

Sanaa said, "'K, cuz you got backup. We're the swoop girls."

"Isn't that supposed to be negative?" Octavia asked.

"No. We're turning it around," Sanaa boasted. "We swoop in and save the day. It might not be easy, but we're turning the whole swoop connotation around."

Olive and Octavia nodded. Then Octavia said, "Has anybody seen Pia?" The other two shook their heads. Bummed, Octavia continued, "Hopefully Ms. Davis will call a meeting soon, and the five of us will have a talk. This bond, this group, this whatever we're forming is only going to work if we all want to be a part of it."

"I'll see you after school," Olive said to Octavia when the bell rang. "Thank you, and hopefully you'll have time to come in and check on our boy."

"I'd like that," Octavia said, happy Olive was finally cool with the fact that she and Shawn liked each other.

Octavia couldn't wait for school to be over. Octavia had been texting Shawn back and forth over the last few days, making sure he was okay. Even though they were really cool, as the school day was ending she got a little nervous. She didn't want to just show up without him expecting her, so she texted him, "Glad ur home, but I wanna check & make sure it's OK if I come by 2 c u. I'm dropping Charles & Olive off."

"Naw, I'd love 2 see u 4 a minute. I'm pretty weak, but seeing u will make me stronger," Shawn texted.

Olive texted back with a smiley face.

Shawn texted back, "Hurry up & get here already."

"R u going to b a good patient 4 me?" Olive texted.

"Ur reading my mind. I plan 2 b real good 4 u 4 sure."

"R u talking dirty 2 me?"

"Me? No," Shawn texted, trying to come off mischievous.

Three hours later Octavia was actually in the room Shawn shared with Charles. Charles gave him privacy with Octavia. Octavia's heart was beating double time.

"Charles didn't say much in the car, only I shouldn't tire you out. He's not too happy with me coming to see you," Octavia shared, breaking the ice.

"No sweat. Charles ain't been happy about much since our house been shot up."

"Yeah, I don't blame him really. He almost lost his boy."

"I don't want to think about that. I'm resilient, so don't mind him. Don't stand all the way over there. Come here."

Octavia was real nervous. She felt something strong for Shawn. When she thought he wasn't going to make it, she couldn't even sleep. Now that they'd been communicating, she wanted to get even closer. Shawn asked her to come closer, but she kept hesitating, like her back was stuck to the door and she couldn't move from it.

"No, I don't want to mess up anything going on with you."

"What's wrong?" Shawn probed as he held out his hand. "I've been thinking about you all day, been waiting for you to get here, and then it seems like you don't want to be here or something. Scared I'ma bite?"

"It's not that," Octavia said, unconscious of the fact that she was moving toward Shawn.

She certainly didn't want to upset him, so her body glided close to his. He tried to sit up from the bed, but he groaned. She got concerned.

"Don't push it," she told him.

"I got stitches, but I'm going to be okay. The bullet is gone. It went in one side and came out the other."

Once she got close enough, Shawn pulled her to him and started trying to kiss her. She backed away, really upset, and said, "I'm sorry. I can't do it."

"Calm down."

"How do you want me to calm down, but you want to kiss me? I can't do both. I can't give you what you want."

"Okay, relax. I don't just want to be with you because of sex."

"Whatever, I'm on the list. I know you think I'm easy."

Offended, Shawn cared enough to explain. "Olive's on the list too. I think the list is stupid. I wanted to kiss you because I wanted to. I don't want you to be uncomfortable. No need to worry. As long as you want to pursue whatever this is, we can take it slow. If anything else is supposed to happen physically between us, it will happen organically."

CHAPTER TEN
Pathetically (Pia's Middle)

Pia was excited that the basketball team lost the first round of the play-offs. She didn't want the basketball team to advance because she now knew that the guys who assaulted her were on the team, plus she was also tired of cheering. She didn't want to quit the squad. So, with the season now over, she was relieved when her coach dropped her off at home.

Pia was also happy to find that there was not a lot of action going on at her house. Most nights her mom and her mom's Mexican girlfriends were throwing house mixers or margarita parties. Sometimes Pia couldn't count on relaxing because too much was going on. But tonight, thankfully, there weren't any lights, and she didn't see any cars in front of their house.

When Pia came in, she yelled, "Mom! I'm home!" But she heard the shower going. Pia put on her nightgown and slipped into bed.

Before she could go to sleep, her cell phone rang. It was Octavia. "Hey, I'm just checking in on you. I heard y'all lost the game. I wanted to make sure you got in alright."

"Oh, that's sweet. Yeah, I'm fine. How's everybody else doing?" Pia asked, caring. She knew she could have done more to stay in touch with the girls over the week, but she'd been distant.

"Everybody's cool. Willow's a little mad at us, but hopefully she'll get over it," Octavia explained.

"Mad at y'all for what?"

"I actually think she's mad at you too."

"Whatever. I'm still mad at myself, so Willow better get in line," Pia said.

"Well, you sound exhausted. I was just gonna call you to get your thoughts on my situation."

"Okay, the way you're talking sounds like you don't wanna let me go to sleep until you get it out, so what's going on, Octavia?"

"It's just Shawn. You know I can't talk to Olive because it's her brother."

"So what's going on with Shawn? Is he okay?" Pia asked with genuine concern.

"Yeah, he's gonna be sore for a while, but the bullet just went through-and-through. He lost a lot of blood at first, but thanks to donors he's recovering. Pia, he's a really sweet guy, and I don't know. I was feeling some type of way for him, and things got a little heated, and . . ."

Assuming where Octavia was going, Pia cut her off and reminded her, "I thought we all agreed we were gonna take things slow with all guys. Please tell me you didn't . . ."

Sensing her friend was getting it all wrong, Octavia laughed and said, "No, no, that's just what I'm saying. He's not trying to pressure me about anything. We kissed. I pulled away. He was fine with it. I'm the one tripping. I don't know. Am I crazy to be excited about him? Is a guy not just wanting me for sex too good to be true? Should I be hopeful about what's growing between me and Shawn?"

"Okay, you asked a bunch of questions. I'm tired, so let me see if I can answer them. First, you are not crazy to be all into him. No, a guy acting like a true gentleman isn't too good to be true. And yes, you can have hope that things could work. The way I see it, coming from where I've just come from, going through what I had to go through, if it's working for you, Octavia, you should embrace it."

"Ooh, I wish I could come through the phone and hug you, Pia! We gotta hang out soon."

"Alright, girl. I'm going to sleep."

The girls said their good-byes. When Pia hung up the phone she realized she cared for her swoop list buddies. They all had been through so much, being the jokes of the school, but hearing Octavia happy made Pia smile.

Pia tried to sleep, but then she heard her door squeaking open. "Mom? I was telling you

I was home, but you were in the shower."

It was weird because her mom did not respond. Pia felt uneasy when she saw a shadowy figure coming closer. She started to cringe when she looked at the figure, and it was not a person with a bunch of hair on her head like her mom. Actually, it looked the opposite, and Pia started to scream. It was a man, and he put his hand around her waist and wouldn't let her get away from him. He pinned her down.

"Get off of me! Stop! Mom! Mom!" Pia yelled out.

"Your mom's not here. She took my car to get some beer. But no need to fear, baby. This is your Uncle Jim."

She remembered Jim, with his bad breath and all. Her mom was supposed to be done with the crazy, lazy dude.

Suddenly, Jim tried to kiss her neck. Pia hated that her purse was so far away because she had a can of mace in it. Quickly, Pia kneed Jim right in the balls, hard. He squealed, and Pia turned on the lights and ran out of her room. She headed toward the front door. Thankfully her mother was coming in.

"Oh my gosh, Mama! You gotta get him outta here!"

"Honey, you know Jim," her mother said calmly.

"Yeah, Mama, and I thought you weren't gonna mess with him anymore."

"Well, I had to pay the rent, sweetie."

"Okay, well hopefully you gave him what you needed to for the rent, but he's gotta go because he's trying to get something from me."

Jim came rushing around the corner. "I don't know what your daughter's telling you, but she's lying. She was screaming and thinking she heard noises. She didn't know it was me. I tried to calm her down, but she kicked me in my private parts."

"Oh my gosh, Pia," her mom said, believing Jim's pitiful excuse and running to his side.

Pia wanted to bash some sense into her mother's fool head, but she knew it wouldn't do any good at all. She had just been groped by her mom's friend, and her mom didn't even pretend to care. Pia dashed to her room and locked her door. In her eyes, her mother was now her enemy. She had hurt her daughter badly and pathetically.

CHAPTER ELEVEN

Judgmentally (Sanaa's End)

"Hey, Pia. What's wrong?" Sanaa asked as they walked into school.

Shaking her head and frowning, Pia gasped, "It's just been a crazy weekend. That's all. I'm not a scholar, but I'm happy to be in school today, that's for sure."

Concerned, Sanaa replied, "What's going on?"

"I don't want you to judge me. No point in even talking about it."

"Why would I judge you? It ain't like my life is all perfect."

Pia stopped walking and asked, "Sanaa, are

you still hiding out from your best friend, not wanting to tell her that the guy she wanted to be her man was yours?"

"You aren't judging me, are you?" Sanaa said, feeling that Pia had her number.

"No, I'm not. I'm being real. Tell the girl and move on."

"One day, but right now I'm trying to see what's up with you." Sanaa placed her hand on Pia's shoulder and asked, "You still dealing with the abortion?"

"Just hearing you saying it like that is hard."

"I know, girl. But I'm here for you. Talk to me."

"This time it's not the whole baby thing. This sleaze my mom was with . . ."

"What?" Sanaa uttered, cutting off Pia. "I know he didn't come on to you?"

"It's my clothes, right?" Pia asked, clearly feeling like the dirty encounter was her fault. "I wear stuff a little too tight. I was asking for it, right? My mom sure took his side."

"No. Don't own any of this. He's just an old fart who needs to get a life. And I'm not trying to talk about your mom, but if she can't understand that, she's the one with the problem."

Sanaa was overwhelmed when Pia reached out and hugged her tight. Pia said, "You just don't know how much I needed that."

When Olive and Octavia walked up together, laughing, Pia pulled apart from Sanaa and tried to get herself together. She didn't want to go into her family drama any more. Trying to be chipper, Pia said, "Look at us. If we go work it out with Willow, the swoop list girls would be friends again."

"Where is Willow?" Olive said. "I'm tired of her being mad at us. She needs to loosen up a bit and understand who are her friends."

"It's obviously not you guys," Willow said, coming from behind them as she sashayed her way on to class.

"Oh no!" Olive said, and she grabbed the back of Willow's shirt. "You coming back here, missy. We're going to talk this thing out."

Willow tugged away. "What's there to talk about? You guys betrayed me. I'm done with kissing behinds."

"You just misunderstood," Sanaa said.

"And you guys are some of the best friends I've ever had," Octavia boldly said. "You included, Willow."

"Please, we're the only friends your red-headed self has ever had," Willow said, getting in a jab on Octavia.

Octavia looked down. Olive looked pissed. Pia looked at them all like *Please settle the heck down.*

Tired of the mounting drama, Sanaa said, "You guys, we can fix this. Willow, just give us a chance. Let us explain why we didn't tell you about the petition to get you kicked off the dance team."

Rolling her eyes, Willow said, "Well, you guys wouldn't understand because you've only been on the swoop list. No one told me about the petition. I could not stop what I didn't know about."

"So, don't let them kick you out of dance," Sanaa said.

"They had over two hundred signatures. I had no choice. My mom and my coach said it was best for me to bow out. I'm not on the dance team anymore."

Sanaa stood beside Willow. She rubbed her back. Willow bluntly pushed by her.

Angry, Willow blurted out, "Don't try to act like you care!"

Getting an attitude back, Sanaa said, "I don't need to try and act like anything. I'm not fake, and I'm not phony."

"You're just keeping a secret from your so-called best friend, but you're not fake or phony? Okay." Willow laughed dead in Sanaa's face.

"You didn't have to say that, Willow. You know the circumstances as to why I'm not dealing with that."

"That doesn't excuse it. If you treating her like that and she's your best friend, how do you think I think you'd treat me? I just don't have no expectations. Get out of my way, y'all!" Willow screamed out as a crowd started staring.

"Just let the evil witch go," Olive said.

Willow turned around and rushed up to Olive, saying, "Heifer, I got your witch."

Unshaken, Olive said, "You the one actin' evil and crazy. What you gon' do?"

Everybody was looking at the five of them fussing at each other. People started shouting, "Zoo animals! Look at the freaks!" or "They're more than just sluts, they're frenemies."

Sanaa was tugged away. When she looked over, it was Miles.

"What are you doing?" Sanaa demanded.

"Wondering what you're doing. Why you still hang out with them? You still want to keep everything quiet from Toni, but it's okay for you to be with these loud girls? The association ain't cool. Obviously they don't want to be with you."

"It was just one girl upset, and she misunderstood some things. It will be alright. Girls do that."

Miles said, "No, it was a big scene of more than one girl upset. Yet you don't want to fuss with Toni and tell her about me? I got to play by your rules, but you can't play by mine? If you want to be with me, we can't do this anymore."

"What? You're giving me an ultimatum that I can't hang out with the swoop list girls?"

Sanaa was pretty pissed at Miles. But maybe he had a point about her still keeping things from Toni. Obviously their friendship had waned. Sanaa didn't want to hurt Toni.

But now Miles wanted her to give up her new friends in order to be with him. As much as Sanaa had been committed to Miles, it was at that moment that she realized he seriously wanted her to dump her new friends.

Sanaa looked at him and said, "I'm sorry. Those girls are my friends."

"But I'm your man," he boldly said.

"Because I gave you another chance."

"Another chance? I told you what you saw wasn't what you thought."

"You keep saying that, but nobody knows that we've been together except you and me, and all of a sudden I show up on the swoop list as some girl who freely gives it up—the first girl on the list."

"You trying to say I put you on the list?"

"Can you honestly say you didn't?"

"I didn't."

"Well, I don't know if I believe you. But I do

know that you're not going to tell me who I can and can't be friends with," Sanaa told him.

"So what are you saying?"

"I'm not giving up my friends. Whatever that means for us, it's what it means," Sanaa boldly stated before walking off. She was tired of Miles looking at her so judgmentally.

CHAPTER TWELVE

Naturally (Willow's End)

"Okay, so why are you actin' all stank?" Sanaa caught up to Willow and asked.

"Excuse me?" Willow turned and abruptly said, rolling her eyes and neck in Sanaa's direction.

"I'm not trying to argue with you or fuss with you anymore, Willow, but I just wanna let you know for real, for real, there's no need to cut out the people who really care. I didn't, and I'm not gonna let you either."

"What are you talking about? I just ended our friendship, in case you don't remember," Willow said.

"Nah, I saw you walk away, but that doesn't mean we aren't friends now."

Willow gave Sanaa a glare, but deep down inside she appreciated the fact that this chick wasn't letting her off the hook. Willow had always been so brash and bold that she never really let her vulnerable side show. But something inside her heart was changing, so she listened intently.

Sanaa shared, "Miles just gave me a crazy ultimatum to drop my friends. But I'm not gonna let Miles tell me who I can and can't be friends with."

"He's got a problem with the swoop list girls because he thinks we're a bunch of suckas bringing his girl down," Willow said, still trying to put on a tough-girl act.

However, Sanaa saw right through the pose and said, "Who cares what he or anybody else thinks? As long as we keep our friendship tight, we'll be fine." She grabbed Willow and hugged her tight. "You are my friend, and if I can prevent something from hurting you, then that's what I'm gonna do.

Don't crucify us because we thought we were doing the right thing. Have a little faith in us."

The old Willow wanted to go off on Sanaa and keep her far away. She wanted to say things that would make her never want to be friends. But the new Willow couldn't deny that she appreciated Sanaa going the extra mile.

Willow let go of her pride and spoke from the bottom of her heart. "I thank you."

"That's better," Sanaa joked with her. "Now I can let you go, see, because I was gonna keep you in a headlock until you stopped tripping."

The two girls started laughing. Willow smiled. "I guess I was being stupid, thinking that y'all hated me and was in a coup with everybody else around here. It's like I lost everything."

"I don't think you lost everything. Look over there in that corner. There's a gentleman who's been checking you out."

"It's just my neighbor, Dawson."

"I know of Dawson Evans. But I also know I've never seen him check out a girl the way he's looking at you."

As Sanaa walked away, Dawson walked over, and Willow's heart started beating a little faster.

"So, you haven't returned my calls," Dawson said to her.

"I haven't really been talking to anybody," Willow uttered, trying to remain unaffected by his attention.

"Why you pulling away?"

"Because you're too good of a guy to mess around with somebody like me."

Dawson replied, "If I cared about what people thought . . ."

"What? You would have never liked me in the first place?"

"Something like that." He shrugged. "But it's not just you. Remember, I'm being raised by a single mom. When I was younger, I got called by a bunch of names. My mom used to always tell me I can't let what people say break me, and so over the years, the more I was put down, the stronger I became. When you go on, live your life, hold your head up high, start believing in yourself, and believe in those who truly care about you, your life can turn around. All I'm saying is, give a brother a chance. I seen the swoop girls, and they seem to be good for you. I wanna be good for you too."

"Oh, you do, huh?" Willow asked in a flirtatious tone before becoming serious. "Even with all my baggage?"

Peering deeply into her eyes, Dawson said, "Let me carry them for you. I can lighten your load, baby."

At that moment, Willow took a real deep breath. She couldn't believe the dude who lived next door, the guy she'd looked past so many years, was now making her heart skip a beat. Dawson had been showing her interest for years, but she was so backwards she never paid attention. Now his strong presence was demanding an audience. He was in her face, straightforward and to the point. He wanted to be her man.

Brushing his lips from her cheek to her ear, he said, "There is a Valentine's Day dance coming up Friday. Go with me?"

"Yes," Willow uttered naturally.

CHAPTER THIRTEEN
Kindly (Olive's End)

With the guys dressed in nice suits and the ladies in adorable, short dresses, Olive smiled as she sat at a table, watching Octavia and Shawn cuddle together, Willow and Dawson laugh at each other, and Sanaa stare at Miles from across the room. Olive wasn't going to let Charles get her down. He was there standing beside her, looking all dapper, but he had an attitude. The Valentine's Day dance was the last place he wanted to be, and he had no problem expressing that she'd basically forced him to be there. When a slow jam came on, couples got up to head to the floor.

Olive leaned in to Sanaa and baited, "Go on, girl, and dance with Miles. Forget Toni. He wants to be with you."

"He drove me here, so that's enough. I'm still letting him stew for trying to make me choose between him and my swoop list girls. But he does look fine, doesn't he? I'ma go stand close to him."

The girls giggled. Before Sanaa walked away, she motioned for Olive to ask Charles. But when Olive saw the mean glare on his face, she just sat there.

Charles looked at Shawn, who was struggling to move, and said, "Bro, you need to sit down somewhere before those stitches pop."

"It's just a slow jam, man. You need to get up and relax a little bit. Get yourself some business and stay out of mine," Shawn jokingly replied as he took Octavia's hand and headed to get his slow groove on.

Charles jerked his shoulders upward in a noncaring way and did not ask Olive to dance. Instead, he sat back with his lips pouted and his arms folded. Even with all that, Olive wasn't going to let Charles spoil her mood. She knew even though he didn't want to be there, he wanted to be with her and that meant so much. It wasn't just what he said, but also what he did that showed his loyalty. He took her to the dance, and even if they sat there all night, she was with a guy who cared about her.

Olive had never had girlfriends to sit with, laugh with, go to the bathroom with, or just do whatever fun, silly stuff that girls did. Now she enjoyed her new friends at the big dance. She had a life and felt so blessed. She just wished Pia was there to share it with them. She wasn't the only one thinking about Pia. All of a sudden, a Hispanic guy tapped her on the shoulder, and Charles rose to his feet. It was Stephen.

"She's with me, man," Charles uttered, having no problem being territorial.

"Naw, man, I'm not trying to cut in. I just wanted to talk to her for a second about one of her friends. I thought since you all weren't dancing, you wouldn't mind if I sat down. For real, I ain't trying to take your girl, man."

"You couldn't," Charles said, feeling the guy out. Satisfied, he calmed his tone. "Alright, cool."

Stephen sat and looked at Olive. "Hey."

"Hey, what's up? You wanted to talk to me?" Olive asked, unsure what he wanted.

"Yeah. I know you've been hanging out with Pia, right?"

"Yeah."

"I'm Stephen Garcia."

"I know who you are. The only good point guard on our basketball team."

Hearing that, Charles perked up. "Yeah, that's right. You shoot hoops for Jackson. Man, I hate y'all didn't keep on doing well for State."

Olive lightly jabbed him in the arm and said, "You had some good shots though."

Charles nodded and said, "You just need some other good jokers around you."

Stephen squinted as he tried to remember Charles. "You're the guy I've seen ballin' in PE. We need to get you out there on the court."

Charles appreciated that Stephen recognized his skills. "If I wasn't a senior, I might just do that."

"We've got some rec and AAU leagues that play this spring."

"Let's hook up then," Charles said as the two hit fists.

"What can I do for you?" Olive cut in.

"Yeah, um, Pia, do you know where she is? Is she here tonight? Did she come with somebody?"

"Actually, she didn't come. We've been calling her. She hasn't returned anybody's calls."

"Mine either. You think she's alright?"

"I don't know. I'm a little worried about her. Seems like you are too."

"I am," Stephen said with true concern on his face.

Unclear, Olive asked, "Were y'all supposed to come together or something?"

"No, no. I mean, I would have brought her if she would have wanted to, but, um . . ."

Still unclear, Olive pried, "So you didn't even ask her?"

"She didn't return my calls."

Getting a tough look from Charles over grilling the guy too much, Olive eased up, "Yeah, okay, you said that. Well, if I hear from her, want me to tell her to call you?"

"I'm thinking about dropping by her place. I'm not a stalker or anything..." Stephen said when he noticed Olive was a little leery at his declaration. "You don't think that would be a good idea?"

Olive threw her hands in the air. "Who am I to say? But I will tell you, if you're feeling you need to reach out, then step out and go by there. I might tell my girls we need to do the same right after the dance. I am a little worried about her."

"Alright, well, thanks," Stephen said as he and Olive stood up and said good-bye.

Olive felt hands around her waist. "Oh, I know you glad I'm at the dance," a voice said.

When she turned around, she jumped back, seeing it was Tiger. She screamed, "Get your hands off of me!"

"I put my hands anywhere I want!" Tiger said as he put both of his hands back around her waist and pulled her close, humping his hips like he was trying to get busy or something.

"You're hurting me! Ouch! Let me go, Tiger!" Olive screamed out.

The next thing she knew, Tiger let go. She turned quickly and was shocked to see Charles with one hand really tight around Tiger's neck. In his other hand was a knife to the side of Tiger's throat.

Charles boldly stated, "You going to disrespect my girl all up in here like this?"

"Your girl?" Tiger teased back. "Please, you can't have what's been and is mine."

Charles tightened the grip and smiled as if he was digging the control. After a few long seconds, Tiger's smirk started fading from his cocky face. The redbone was turning purple.

"You got to let him go, Charles," Olive pleaded.

Before she could get through to him, administrators and the cops on duty pulled Charles off of Tiger. Immediately, they put him on the floor and put him in handcuffs. Olive became hysterical as they carried Charles towards the exit. Sanaa noticed what was going on and wrapped her arms around Olive, trying to comfort her.

"Oh my gosh. Oh my gosh!" Olive shouted.

"It's going to be okay!" Sanaa said, holding on to her friend.

Olive broke free from Sanaa and ran over to the police officer and shouted, "You've got to let him go. You don't understand. He was protecting me!"

The officer frowned with no remorse and said, "Young lady, this boy had a knife on school premises. To that type of violence we don't take too kindly."

CHAPTER FOURTEEN

Believably (Octavia's End)

Octavia had never been on the dance floor with a guy's arms draped around her waist. She'd never been rocked back and forth with such care and concern. She had never felt so relaxed. At first she was worried about Shawn's health, feeling that he shouldn't even be out. However, he'd put her mind at ease, telling her he knew the significance of this dance for her and that he wasn't going to miss it. Just as she was about to tell him how much she appreciated him for going the extra mile for her, he pulled away, all upset.

"What— What's wrong?" Octavia asked,

bummed that he'd tugged away.

He turned Octavia around and pointed to the mayhem ensuing on the other side of the dance floor. "It's Charles. I don't see him anywhere."

"He probably took off with Olive."

"No, look at Tiger's crew. Look at everybody all in an uproar. Something's going on. There's policemen over there. Where's Charles?" Shawn jerked away too aggressively and got a sharp pain in his side.

Helping him sit down, Octavia declared, "You are not going anywhere! Let me go find out what's going on with him."

"Hurry back!" Shawn told her.

"Willow, will you please watch out for him?" Octavia asked her girlfriend.

"Fo' sho'. I got it, girl. Go!"

Octavia didn't want to leave a hurting Shawn, but Willow pushed and nudged her to go. Octavia reluctantly took off towards the commotion. All the people were by the front door of the school, and that's where Octavia found Olive and Sanaa.

"What the heck is going on?" Octavia questioned, seeing Olive being consoled by Sanaa.

Olive lifted up her head from Sanaa's shoulder and said, "They got Charles! They're taking him to jail!"

"For what?" Octavia asked, dumbfounded, like that was the most stupid news she'd ever heard.

"He had a knife," Sanaa tried whispering. She didn't want to get Olive more upset than she was from hearing the truth.

"But Tiger's still here. Clearly, he did something too. This isn't fair," Olive replied, more upset anyway.

Octavia squinted. "I don't understand."

"Exactly," Olive yelled, feeling no justice. "Tiger's got some of those policemen paid. It probably is just a couple, but a couple is all it takes. It ain't right, but it's real. I got to get to the police station. Somebody's gotta help me. I gotta get Ms. B. Where's Shawn?"

Before Olive could take off to find Shawn, Octavia knew she was going to have to have it out with her girlfriend. So Octavia stood in Olive's way and said, "Listen, this is like déjà vu in my head. Last month in the cafeteria, you and Shawn desperately wanted to have Charles's back. We all thought Charles might get shot, but Shawn was the one who got shot a month later. He is weak. He shouldn't even be here tonight, but he came anyway. Listen, you can't go to him, Olive. It won't be good for him to learn of this. He could end up right back in the hospital. Please don't go over there."

Olive glared Octavia's way. Octavia's stomach had butterflies. She didn't want to back down, nor did she want confrontation with her friend. But if she had to show her she was serious and continue to stand her ground, she would.

She was actually surprised when Olive said, "You're right. You make sense. I'll get Sanaa to take me. You didn't drive."

"Right," Octavia said, wishing Olive would go alone. "I'll be fine."

"I know, but get Willow to get Dawson to take you and Shawn home."

Octavia nodded, but before Olive could jet, she grabbed her friend's wrist. "But Shawn is gon' ask all kinds of questions. I don't wanna lie to him."

"Well, you can't have it both ways, Octavia. Figure it out, but don't stress him out," Olive asserted.

Octavia agreed. The two girls hugged. Then they went their separate ways to take care of business.

As soon as Shawn saw Octavia coming, he struggled but still stood up. "Where . . . where is he? What . . . what's going on with him?"

"I've arranged to get you home."

"What are you talking about? Where's Charles? And look, don't feed me no bull."

"You don't need to get upset, Shawn."

"Octavia, I like you. You know that, but this is my family. I'm not a kid."

"Yeah, but you're hurt. If you get upset, you could end up back in the hospital. Then how could I live with myself, knowing you would not have even been here if you didn't have to escort me tonight?"

"If something's happening to Charles and I don't know . . ."

Seeing his temples swell with anger, Octavia conceded. "Okay, okay! He's gone to jail."

"What!?" Shawn exclaimed with disdain.

"But we can't go there. You gotta go home," Octavia stated. She looked at Willow. "Could you please help me?"

"Shawn, you can't even stand up, man. You ain't gon' do Charles or nobody any good. You can hate me forever, but I'm not having you dropped off at jail."

"You know what? Just get me home."

Willow talked to Dawson. They got Dawson's car, and the four of them drove to the group home. All the while they were driving, Octavia sensed Shawn's anger towards her. She wanted to beg him to understand, but at the end of the day, she knew it was better that he hate her for the rest of her life than she allow him to stress himself into a coma. When they got to the group home, no one was there. Ms. B had already left.

"See what you've done? I've missed them.

I should have gone to the jail," he snarled at Octavia.

"I'm sorry you're mad at me. Understand this is what Charles would want. Why can't you go relax like we all need to do? Charles wouldn't want you stressed."

Shawn rolled his eyes and said, "You don't even know Charles. You don't know what he'd want. I'm supposed to be there for him. I'm supposed to have his back. If he's in jail, I'm supposed to be in jail too."

"You took a bullet that was probably for him! You took that! You've already done enough! You can barely even stand now. You shouldn't have been out at all. What if something happens to you, Shawn? Finally, I get a guy who comes in my life and cares about me, and you think I wanna just let you go out and get in harm's way? Are you serious? I care about you, can't you see?" Octavia said in an emotional way.

Sensing how much she cared, Shawn took her in his arms and held her tight. "I'm sorry. I'll settle down. I don't have any doubts that you care about me. Not only are you telling me so, but your actions are showing it so believably."

CHAPTER FIFTEEN
Earnestly (Pia's Ending)

"Mom, wake up!" Pia shouted the night of the Valentine's Day dance.

She didn't know what kind of drugs her mom had taken, but she was unresponsive. Pia knew she wasn't dead because she had a pulse. But Pia was scared.

"What did you give my mother?" she yelled at Jim as she pounded on his chest.

"Oh, I love you feisty! But I'm getting what I paid for tonight! Your momma can't, so I'm taking it from you," Jim said as he pushed Pia down and started ripping off her pants.

Pia wrestled to get Jim off. However, he was

too fat to move. Pia used her determination and wits. As soon as Jim wiggled to undo his pants, Pia squeezed him in the groin. He squealed and rolled off. Seizing the moment, she got up and dashed out of the house. She ran so fast into the street she nearly got hit by a car.

The car screeched to a stop. That's when Pia noticed Stephen from school in the driver's seat. She frantically howled, "Help!"

He left his car in the middle of the road, came over to her, and asked, "What's wrong?"

Jim came charging out of the house. "You get away, boy. She's mine!"

Stephen moved Pia behind him. He knew he was going to have to do what he hadn't done a couple months before, and that was stand up for the girl he cared about. He wasn't going to let anyone violate her again. He dared the drunk slob to try him.

"Told your momma you was fast anyway," Jim blurted out, backing down before he headed back inside.

"I can't stay here tonight," Pia cried out, placing her head on Stephen's chest.

"Don't worry. I got you," Stephen said as he hugged her.

Stephen pointed toward her zipper. She hadn't even noticed that her clothes were mangled. As she fixed herself, she got in his car.

"Shucks, my cell is inside. I can't go in there. Please just take me to Willow's!"

"Okay, but they are at the dance."

"She went to the dance? I hadn't even talked to them in a long time. What am I thinking? I can't go over there."

"They were worried about you. You can use my phone to call. Trust me, they need you. It got crazy."

"What do you mean?" Pia asked, getting worried.

"I don't know all the details, but I got a hunch your girls will be getting together tonight."

Stephen took Pia over to Willow's house, but she wasn't home yet. They stayed in Stephen's car and waited. Stephen asked, "You okay?"

Frustrated, Pia said, "Heck naw, I'm not okay. You know I was raped by your basketball buddies. They're walking around scot-free like they've done nothing."

"All you've got to do is say the word," Stephen declared. "I'll back you up."

Pia threw up her hands. "But for what? For you to get ostracized? For them to dismiss my claim because I waited to tell? Forget it. You've helped me enough tonight. Thank you for being there."

"Does your mom know her boyfriend is like that?" Stephen blurted out.

Pia pondered for a moment and then decided to let down her guard. She said, "Yes. She doesn't care. I was locked in my room, and I thought I was fine, but I heard some stumbling. I heard her talking, then she wasn't talking anymore, so I came out to make sure she was okay. She was passed out! I don't know if he slipped something in her drink to get with me, or if she just doesn't care. She didn't believe me when I told her last time. Or even if she really does know what's going on, as long as we get a dollar to pay the rent, she's fine. What a great mom I have."

"Don't beat yourself up. It's hard trying to

make it out here. People just doing the best they can. But you're strong."

"So strong that I'm all torn apart."

"So what? You're surviving. You're making it through. Just like with basketball, you might get down some shots, but you don't give up until the buzzer rings. You're still in the game, Pia."

"Urgh, I don't need any kind of lesson right now."

Stephen shook his head. He wanted to pull her close and tell her all would be alright. However, he could tell he was pushing her away.

"Sorry," Pia said, seeing his head drop. "I didn't mean to snap. You're just trying to help me."

"I was hoping you'd be at the dance tonight," he said, trying to connect.

"Really?"

"Yeah. I got all spiffy so I could give you a twirl. Olive told me she thought you were home."

"So you just dropped by?"

"Crazy, right?"

"You don't have to feel bad, ya know."

"Bad about what?" Stephen asked her.

"Feeling like you've got to be my hero now because you didn't stop those guys from raping me."

"Well, I can't turn off how I feel. I didn't man up then. I won't make that mistake again. I promise you that," Stephen emphatically stated.

"I believe you."

Pia was so happy to see Willow pull up in Dawson's car. Willow said goodnight to Dawson and thanked him for taking her to the dance.

When Willow got out of the passenger's side, Octavia popped out from the backseat. Pia ran over to them and explained all that had happened.

"You're staying with me," Willow said.

Pia was so grateful. Without a stitch of clothes, toothbrush, or anything personal, at least she had a place to lay her head for the night. Willow's friendship meant so much.

"Sorry I've been distant, but . . ."

"You've been trying to take care of you," Willow said.

"I'm glad you knew we have to stick together so we can help take care of each other."

Pia went and told Stephen she was okay. He asked if he could call her sometime. She said she wasn't sure. He seemed like he didn't want to take no for an answer, but he drove away anyway.

"He likes you," Willow said when Pia came back to her friends.

"Can't even focus on that. I was almost raped by my mom's boyfriend."

Octavia chimed in, "The night's been tough. Shawn wanted to end up back in the hospital."

"Yeah, but you talked him out of it," Willow said.

As the three walked towards the house, Sanaa and Olive pulled up. The girls were excited to have another sleepover. It had only been a couple weeks since the last one, but they needed more girl time to talk after all they'd been through that night. They realized they didn't have much faith in a lot going on, but they decided they needed to have faith in each other and believe in something. After they were steeled, they reflected on their craziness.

Willow said, "I want to read y'all something.

I shared this with Sanaa when y'all were here the last time. It's crazy because that Leah girl . . ."

"Who?" Olive asked.

Willow said, "The girl who's dead who keeps writing us. She claims she used to be on the swoop list at another school, but she got so sick of everybody that she committed suicide over it."

"How could a dead girl write?" Pia asked.

"I don't know, but we've got to find out. I do know she had good points in both letters." Willow showed them the note. "We're on to something with this whole faith thing. We already said we were going to clean up our acts. Now we got to believe life is going to get better. And I'm sorry I pulled away over the petition y'all didn't tell me about."

"Yeah, and I pulled away too," Pia admitted.

"No worries, that's over. Now, my problem is what's gonna happen to Charles," Olive said. "He's locked up for the night, and there is nothing I can do."

"You can stop worrying and believe he's going to be okay," Sanaa said. "I'm going to believe I'll find the courage to tell Toni the whole story."

"You can," Willow said, "And I'm excited to believe in me. It's not what people say about me that controls my outcome, but what I learn from my tough times that make me wiser."

"I get that," Olive uttered. "I know revenge won't solve anything. And I'm believing I can get the ones I care about to understand that too. Thanks, Octavia, for really looking out for Shawn. Sorry I doubted you'd be good for him."

Octavia reached out and hugged Olive tight. "I always thought you had to conform to be with the 'in' crowd. I now know when you believe in something bigger than yourself to work it out, things will work out. You all like me for me."

Pia listened intently and needed to share. "You all are making me stronger. Not sure what's going to happen with my mom and me. My world is upside down, but I wanted to turn to you all for help. I believe in us."

The rest of the night the girls cried,

laughed, and shared even more of their hearts. All wasn't right in their worlds, but for the moment, because they had each other, all was right in their hearts. They all were thankful their friendship was true, genuine, and budding earnestly.

ACKNOWLEDGMENTS

On your knees . . . we all can use some humility. If you're having trouble believing in yourself, get some faith! Placing your hope above propels you forward. Here's gigantic thanks to the folks who keep me believing in myself.

To my parents, Dr. Franklin and Shirley Perry, thank you for allowing me to believe in my dreams. You helped me to know with God all things are possible. To my extended family, thank you for telling me to believe in my talents. Your help in spreading the word about my books means so much. To my assistants Ashely Cheathum, Alyxandra Pinkston, and Candace Johnson, thank you for believing in deadlines. Your work ethic is a blessing. To my dear friends, thank you for helping me believe I've got worth. Your friendships make me wiser. To my teens, Dustyn, Sydni, and Sheldyn, thank you believing in my values. Being your mom makes me desire high standards for your lives. To my husband, Derrick, thank you for believing in our love. These last twenty years I've been your Pud, you've surely been there for me. To my readers, especially the kids in Jackson, GA, who gave me the idea for the series, thank you for believing in what's right. Your care for others helped me to see the true need for these books. And to my Redeemer, thank you for believing in me. When I get down, you always show up and show me my writing career is in Your will. Thank you for that gift.

ABOUT THE AUTHOR

STEPHANIE PERRY MOORE is the author of more than sixty young adult titles, including the Sharp Sisters series, the Grovehill Giants series, the Lockwood Lions series, the Payton Skky series, the Laurel Shadrach series, the Perry Skky Jr. series, the Yasmin Peace series, the Faith Thomas Novelzine series, the Carmen Browne series, the Morgan Love series, the Alec London series, and the Beta Gamma Pi series. Mrs. Moore is a motivational speaker who enjoys encouraging young people to achieve every attainable dream. She lives in the greater Atlanta area with her husband, Derrick, and their three children. Visit her website at www.stephanieperrymoore.com.

READ ALL THE BOOKS IN THE
SWOOP LIST SERIES:

STEPHANIE PERRY MOORE

THE SWOOP LIST SANNA
GIVE IT UP

STEPHANIE PERRY MOORE

THE SWOOP LIST WILLOW
ON YOUR KNEES

STEPHANIE PERRY MOORE

THE SWOOP LIST OLIVE
BACK THAT THING

STEPHANIE PERRY MOORE

THE SWOOP LIST OCTAVIA
FEEL REAL GOOD

STEPHANIE PERRY MOORE

THE SWOOP LIST PIA
SIT ON TOP

THE **SHARP** SISTERS

Make Something of It

STEPHANIE PERRY MOORE

Better Than Picture Perfect

STEPHANIE PERRY MOORE

Turn Up for Real

STEPHANIE PERRY MOORE

Truth and Nothing But

STEPHANIE PERRY MOORE

Icing on the Cake

STEPHANIE PERRY MOORE